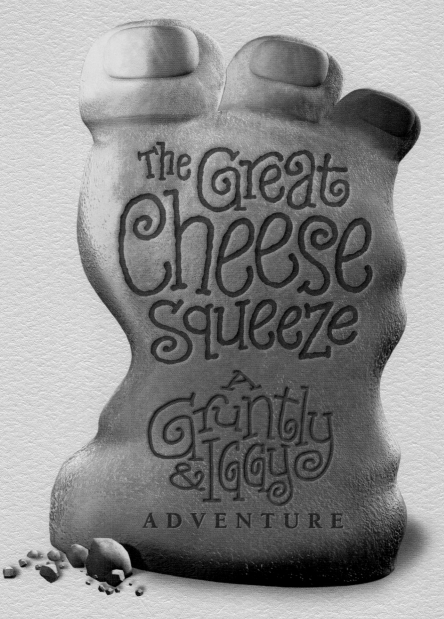

The Great Cheese Squeeze

A Gruntly & Iggy Adventure

written and illustrated by Bryan Ballinger and Keith Lango

BIG IDEA BOOKS™

Zonderkidz

www.bigidea.com

Zonder**kidz**™

The children's group of Zondervan

www.zonderkidz.com

The Great Cheeze Squeeze
ISBN: 0-310-70506-1
Text and Illustrations copyright © 2002 by Bryan Ballinger and Keith Lango
Requests for information should be addressed to:
Zonderkidz, Grand Rapids, Michigan 49530

Editor: Cindy Kenney, Gwen Ellis
Interior Design and Art Direction: Bryan Ballinger and Keith Lango

Printed in the United States
02 03 04 05/PC/4 3 2 1

Two people are better than one.
They can help each other in everything they do.

Ecclesiastes 4:9, NIrV

Bryan and Keith would like to thank:

Chris Meidl, Phil Vischer, Ron Eddy, Kim, Jen,
Laura Bean, Candice, Merrill, Al and Sue,
Betsy and Lowell, and Bob Starnes.

This book is dedicated to both our dads,
Lowell Ballinger and Al Lango, who have passed on to glory.

Standing tall and proud on the prairie was the lighthouse home of Mr.Gruntly Fromage and the Reverend Ignatious P. Bumblesmog. These two friends took pride in a job well done, for no ship had ever crashed there.

When they weren't busy with lighthouse duties, Gruntly and Iggy liked to keep busy. Gruntly would tinker away in his workshop and make sculptures of his favorite subject—toes. He was so fond of toes that he wished to share his love of the bumpy, pudgy digits through his art. So he carved stubby masterpieces out of cheese, knowing there was no finer material than cheese for crafting such irresistible wigglies.

Likewise, Iggy, a country preacher, enjoyed creating wind chimes from buggy bits. Dragonfly wings, beetle feet, grasshopper legs, and such—all collected from his dinner leftovers—filled his hobby room. He was a frugal frog who saw a new wind chime in everything creepy and crawly.

Together Gruntly and Iggy would sell their crafts in the lighthouse gift shop, for many tourists came to see the only lighthouse on the prairie.

Ye Olde
LightHouse
Shoppe

Purveyors of
Fine Cheese Sculptures
& Entymological Windchimes

One day the two friends were enjoying a meal and some fellowship. Gruntly was horking down his favorite food—cheese-filled hot dogs—and reading a magazine. Iggy was preparing some dragonfly tea and thorax nibblers. "Whatcha reading, Gruntly?" he asked.

"Oh, I'm just looking over this issue of Cheese Digest for ideas. The Prairie Cheese Carvers' contest is coming up." Just then Gruntly noticed a hint of a strange smell wafting through the kitchen. Gruntly wrinkled his nose, wondering where the stinkiness was coming from. "Are you going to enter one of your cheddar toes in the contest?" asked Iggy.

Gruntly was distracted from his sniffing by Iggy's question. "Huh? Oh! Well, I want to try something unique. Everybody carves with mozzarella or Gorgonzola, but I'd like to really wow 'em this year."

"Oh," mumbled Iggy, wondering what a Gorgonzola was anyway. "Well, if you need a hand, let me know," Iggy said aloud. No, no, I've got it," dismissed Gruntly.

Gruntly returned to his reading and turned a page, looking for cheesy ideas. But without knowing it, he knocked a cheese dog onto Iggy's chair. When Iggy was ready to enjoy his meal, he sat down right on the cheese dog, which made a horrifying "SPLATCHOOIE!" sound. Immediately, Iggy vaulted out of his chair, hitting his head on the ceiling. Left smooshed onto his chair was a very flat hot dog, which obviously had been no match for his bottom.

An upset Iggy left the kitchen. He was still sore from sitting on a hot cheese soufflé the night before...and now this! He hated sitting on food; he always had.

Gruntly grabbed a spatula to scrape the hot dog off Iggy's chair. Then he stopped. Where was the cheese? He instantly caught sight of a big blob of goo on the fridge. The cheese! When Iggy sat on the cheese dog, the cheese must have squirted out. Pulling it off the fridge, Gruntly noticed the cheese felt like clay. As he mushed it around on a plate, he shouted "Eureka! I've found the perfect cheese!"

Gruntly rushed upstairs with excitement in his heart and a load of cheese dogs in his arms. All that night he fastened and hammered, glued and screwed, 'til his weary eyes drooped into slumber.

Iggy worked on a wind chime down in his room. As he glued a bee wing to a centipede, his nostrils began to twitch. "What is that unspeakable stench? Why, I believe it's coming from my socks!"

Iggy loved to wear woolen socks to keep his frippery feet warm as he tromped through bogs, looking for buggy bits. But he often forgot to wear shoes, and he hadn't changed his socks for weeks! So Iggy's stockings had turned sour, stinking beyond the ability of even a frog to endure. (And that is really something since frogs are rather poor sniffers.) Even his wind chimes were shriveling under the blistering reek of those rotting socks.

Fortunately Iggy had a most clever plan. He quickly doffed his socks, put them and the rest of his overripe laundry into a container, and crammed the whole mess into the freezer. Surely frozen clothes wouldn't smell as bad. "Boy," said Iggy, "we're gonna have to buy another freezer. This one's pretty stuffed!" He then toddled off to bed.

The next morning Iggy was eager for another bug hunt. But when he opened his sock drawer, he found that it was empty! How could he venture forth if the dew was allowed to run freely over his webby digits? Frantic, he felt around the back of the drawer with his tongue. All he found was a dust bunny and an old cobweb, neither of which were socks, nor did they taste very good. After washing his tongue under the faucet, Iggy went to ask Gruntly if he could borrow a pair of socks.

Sound asleep in his workshop, Gruntly was resting next to a very peculiar machine. "What in the world is that?" thought Iggy. Then his eye caught a pile of sad-looking, squished cheese dogs.

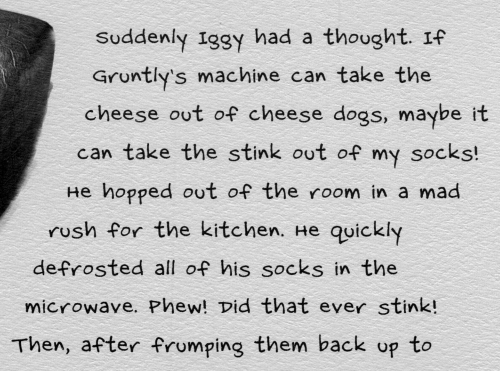

Suddenly Iggy had a thought. If Gruntly's machine can take the cheese out of cheese dogs, maybe it can take the stink out of my socks! He hopped out of the room in a mad rush for the kitchen. He quickly defrosted all of his socks in the microwave. Phew! Did that ever stink! Then, after frumping them back up to Gruntly's room, he slopped the drip-droppy socks into Gruntly's machine. He threw the switch and stood back. Soon the clack and slurp of the world's only Decheesinator echoed across the prairie.

The socks came out smelling only half bad! So Iggy ran them through a few more times until they only faintly stunk. Then he neatly folded his freshly-squeezed socks, and carried them off. He was looking forward to his bug-hunting trek with less stinky stockings on his feet.

That afternoon Gruntly finally awoke, dizzy with excitement. Hauling out the cheese dogs, he dumped them into his machine. After turning it on, he left for a late breakfast. He returned to find a very nice heap of freshly squeezed cheese-dog cheese. But suddenly, his whiskers started to wilt for the cheese smelled horribly foul! Gruntly realized something. "There's only one smell that makes my throat burn and my tummy turn like this." That's when Gruntly noticed something in the bin that did not belong there—one of Iggy's socks!

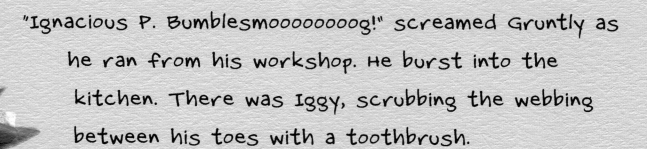

"Ignacious P. Bumblesmoooooooog!" screamed Gruntly as he ran from his workshop. He burst into the kitchen. There was Iggy, scrubbing the webbing between his toes with a toothbrush.

"Did you force your fetid socks through my Decheesinator?" cried Gruntly.

"Umm, maybe...I mean, well...I just kinda figured it was the thing to do. And it really took the stink out of them too!" he nodded. "Well, most of it...Well, some of it anyway."

Gruntly was shaking with fury. "Do you realize what you've done? Now all my cheese smells like stinky feet!"

Iggy cowered behind his chair as Gruntly continued. "How will it look when I put my cheese toes in the competition and they...smell...like...feet?" Gruntly stopped.

"Wait a minute!" he exclaimed. "I have an idea. Think about it—cheese toes that actually smell like real feet!"

Amazed, Iggy looked up at a smiling, happy Gruntly.

"Why, I bet that all the other carvings in the contest will smell just like plain old cheese. That's certainly not very interesting," said Gruntly.

"No, I don't suppose it is," smiled a quite-relieved Iggy.

So Gruntly went ahead and sculpted those stinky cheese toes. He put them in the contest and they won the "Most Original" ribbon at the Prairie Cheese Carvers' Competition.

After the contest, Gruntly turned to Iggy and said, "And to think, if it hadn't been for you and your stinky socks, I never would have won."

Iggy smiled. "And if it hadn't been for your Decheesinator, we would have had to buy a new freezer!"